MEET THE FAMILY

First published in Great Britain in 2022 by Andersen Press Ltd.,

20 Vauxhall Bridge Road, London, SW1V 2SA, UK · Vijverlaan 48, 3062 HL Rotterdam, Nederland

Text copyright © John Yeoman, 1993, 2022 (abridged). Illustration copyright © Quentin Blake, 2022.

Text first published by Hamish Hamilton in 1993 in The Family Album.

1   3   5   7   9   10   8   6   4   2

Printed and bound in China.

British Library Cataloguing in Publication Data available.

Hardback ISBN 978 1 83913 012 0

Paperback ISBN 978 1 83913 096 0

MEET THE FAMILY

words by John Yeoman

pictures by Quentin Blake

ANDERSEN PRESS

The item should be returned or renewed by the last date stamped below.

Dylid dychwelyd neu adnewyddu'r eitem erbyn y dyddiad olaf sydd wedi'i stampio isod.

PILLGWENLLY

To renew visit / Adnewyddwch ar
www.newport.gov.uk/libraries

Our Uncle Marvello and Auntie Shazam
(To tell you the truth, they're just Eric and Pam)
Will always amaze you, whenever you go,
By giving their magical mystery show.

They take off their top hats and peel off their gloves
And, waving their wands, produce dozens of doves;

They conjure up flowers, and rabbits, and spoons,
And fill the whole room up with dancing balloons.

He makes someone's wallet and watch disappear,
And pulls out a long string of flags from your ear.
She smiles from her box with the swords sticking through,
And gives us a wave while he saws her in two.

And just when you're really enjoying the joke
They've suddenly gone in a puff of blue smoke.

Although Baby Cedric is too young to talk,
Or read, or play football, or whistle, or walk,
He doesn't just sit there. Oh, no, not at all:
He might not know much, but he knows how to crawl.

He scuttles up curtains; he skims across floors;
He's surely the speediest thing on all fours.

He won't be imprisoned in playpen or cot:
The top of the wardrobe's his favourite spot.

He's quiet as a kitten, and ten times as fast.
Thank goodness we always retrieve him at last!

Although Cousin Charlie is only just ten,
He's lived in the kitchen since goodness knows when.

His rich chocolate sponges, his golden fruit pies
And Viennese pastries have won every prize.
We peep through the window and thrill to the sight
Of marzipan slices, and strawberry delight,

And apricot crumble, and roast almond flakes,
And caramel custard, and cinnamon cakes,
And raspberry trifles, and fancy iced tarts,
And coconut fingers, and gingerbread hearts,
And no end of puddings, all served piping hot.

It seems such a shame that he eats the whole lot.

Aunt Lorna's five daughters, be-ribboned and frilled,
Are slim and athletic, and terribly skilled:

Secure on their trolley they juggle with bread;
The youngest piles seventeen cans on her head.

They scoop up bananas and cartons of cream,
This prize-winning Superstore Balancing Team.

They do a week's shopping in ten minutes flat –

Unless they bump into the manager's cat!

We call round to visit, whenever we can,
Our Uncle Ignatius and Auntie Diane.

They keep heaps of costumes inside an old chest;
We're always surprised at the way that they're dressed:

They're pirates,

or pixies,

or firemen,

or flies –
They really have mastered the art of disguise.

Our Auntie Amanda is light on her feet;
The people applaud when she twirls down the street.

She keeps a big trap which she sprinkles with rice
And catches no end of inquisitive mice.

She takes them out gently by lifting the flap,

And teaches them ballet,

and Latin,

and tap.

Belinda and Hattie, our elderly aunts,
Have crammed their whole house with extravagant plants.
They polish the leaves and they chat to each bloom
And they water the flowerpots that fill every room.

But just for a change, every once in a while,
They look at each other and give a sly smile,
And hitch up their dresses and fling off their capes,

And swing through the leaves like a couple of apes.